White Girl

(or a Treatise on No' Mo Empathy for Black Folk During the Crack-Era)

A short story by: Sparrow (Jesse Lane)

White Girl
Sparrow (Jesse Lane)

White Girl
Sparrow (Jesse Lane)

White Girl
Sparrow (Jesse Lane)

For J. and the world that escapes through their vices, but not from them.

White Girl
Sparrow (Jesse Lane)

A white girl leaned over to his small nightstand table dipping her face and letting the tip of her nose hang above a line of equally white powder. He watched her. She rocked her head back and forth with a soft cadence as she drew up from the dark wood. He could feel his blood warm and shook his sheets from his ebon-stained skin. Her eyes widened and he thought of his father.

"You sure you don't want some?" she turned and asked him, wiping at her right nostril.

"I'm sure." he replies. Softly leaning back... he attempted to shake his father from his thoughts while looking at her. He thought of another girl instead, a girl that wouldn't place her amber-polished fingers in the remnant grains of cocaine on the table to stick them in her mouth.

"My gums are numb," she proclaimed proudly, her thin lips revealing a childlike grin.

He wasn't amused, but luckily wasn't the type to wear his indifference pointedly on his face, so when his lips didn't curl and his brow didn't furl, the white girl leaned over and placed her lips on his, and he discovered it was vain…. thoughts of his father would persist . They were fragmented little things, scenes with no mise en scène to guide them—just the shallow pull of one memory into the next:

His father standing alone in his childhood home, gaunt and tall.

A harmonica in his hands, and the scorned metal wailing of trains.

His father getting him McDonalds.

His father denying him McDonalds.

Heat rising from Sunday dinner his grandmother had made and his father falling asleep after the meal...

He pulled away from her and could feel heat retreating from between his thighs. His father, a haunt that made the room cold. She stared at him sniffling, eyes even wider now.

“Am I doing something wrong?” she asked.

“No, you aren’t he, placates,” it’s just me… I took too many pills,” he lies. He didn’t take any that day, explicitly for that reason. *Was there a name for whiskey-dick, but with pills?* he thought. He wanted to want her; it was just his father, the memories invasive and without end, drew him away from her. He thought of ways to dismiss her but couldn’t and ended up excusing himself to the bathroom where he actually kept his pills. He crushed up one of them into a neat little line the same way she had earlier on his table, only to realize he didn't have a dollar to snort with, gave up, and tied up the powder in some toilet paper to parachute later, before hiding it in the counter above him.

He returned to her solemn.

"You okay?" she asks.

"Yes," he replies, climbing onto the bed and grabbing her legs parting them some.

"Is it ok?" He asks, throwing his head up onto her belly-button, planting a subtle kiss.

She chuckles, grabbing at his dreads and pushing my head downward, "Go to work," she consented.

He did, his tongue painting small circles around the swell of her clit every now and then, dipping inside of her. Her breath grew more concussive, rapid, and desperate as he did, but she didn't moan. He felt assured and confident in himself now, kissing the fold of her lips—warm and plush, the flappy flesh caressing his moustache as he lunged back and forth.

All of it held a type of rhythm—a sort of jazz that built upon itself as the minutes carried on. He started to find himself improvising now, but was discouraged when he looked upward to find her stare cast toward the dimly lit ceiling and not him. He decided to stop, slowly easing his finger out of her.

“Why did you stop?”

“I thought you didn’t like it,” he said, wiping at his mouth.

She wiped at her nose sniffing. “I loved it; it felt good,” lips pursed displaying her disappointment, but choosing to reassure him anyways.

“Your nigga is gonna kill me,” he told her.

“Darius?” she scrunched her face, rolling her eyes. “He’s not gonna do shit.”

“I don’t know, you all are a bit more in this shit than I am.”

“You deal fucking fucking H,” she snapped, “we only move blow. Trust me you got some way heavier shit going on, Lee.”

Maybe it was true, and maybe he did. He had never given it much thought. A couple of J's here and there— banging their dope, sniffing their dope, crushing up some fentanyl analogues in the public library bathroom never amounted much to him. Just a bunch of white boys. He only sold his shit to white boys. White boys were entitled to everything.

"Don't worry about Dee so much... he doesn't know about you and never will... "plus, if the nigga was doing his job, I wouldn't even be here with you, "she promised slyly.

"Don't fucking say that," near instinctually, he snapped. His teeth grinding against one another; the white glint of his jaw polished itself on violence and anger in that moment, the word gnawing just as much at him as he seemed to be upon himself.

Her eyes watered. He looked at her with a deadpan stare and could tell that he scared her. Admittedly, he wanted it that way. He wasn't going to have some white girl saying "nigga" around him so casually. She cast her eyes downward and apologized to the sheets on the bed.

"It's okay, just a pet peeve of mine."

"I forgot," she lies.

"It's alright just forget it."

Silence filled his bedroom, and he began to feel as equally sparse and meager. He knew he could replace that space; the space between he and Hannah with fentanyl. He quickly excused himself to the bathroom once more, where a blue pill split seamlessly into two. He stared down at where his midnight skin had to recede gracefully away from the edges of his palm but he could tell it craved the azul small half-moon he held out openly before him.

How fast do I want this to hit? He thought. He thought about crushing the half on the bathroom sink where the blue powder would bleed out onto the ivory sink in one skinny, veiny line. He loved the expediency of snorting, but couldn't find it in him, to liken himself to Hannah and the whiteboys he sold to. In his mind, they were like infants. They were always the ones who needed instant gratification. That wasn't him. He ended up swallowing it whole. He didn’t fuck with his own supply often, but felt he needed the mellow warmth the opiates provided right now. Having Hannah over made him tense this night in a way he hadn’t felt before with her. He wasn’t intimidated by the thought of her boyfriend discovering her infidelity, and he wasn’t put off by her doing blow at his place (she did often). It was something much deeper than that, something foreign to it all yet somehow familiar to him, intrinsic even.

He could feel his father gnawing at him again.

When he returned to his room, he found Hannah lying in the same spot he left her, only she had her face in her phone now. The room felt grim and heavier than before, and he prayed the pill would kick in soon. Even orally, fentanyl didn’t take this long to kick in. *Maybe my nerves are keeping it from working,* he thought. He stood at the foot of his bed looking down on her before crawling over the sheets to nuzzle up beside her, hoping that in laying down, the high would hit.

It did.

"Hey…" Hannah started up, placing her phone on the night-stand," …have you wrote any new poems?" she asked.

He nodded sluggishly, the weight in the room beginning to lift a bit.

"Not forreal," he replied, "I tried writing one bout…" he couldn't finish the sentence and began to nod off his head falling onto her shoulder like a child looking to be comforted by his mother before bed-time.

"Are you high?" she asked curiously.

"Yeah," he murmured, barely parting his lips.

"H?"

"Hell-nah— I sell that shit; I don't fuck with it," he slurred raggedly, anger bringing him out of his nod some, "I just popped half of a pressed blue."

"Ohhh. Haha, You sure you should be doing more pills?" she replied.

He stared at her a while, studying her face, trying to quell some of his annoyance over her pointless inquiries. He wanted to give himself over to something good. He wanted her to compliment his high, but right now, her words felt antagonistic and he couldn't explain why. He looked into her brown eyes, her pupils dilated, and wondered if she saw more than he did somehow, If so, he wasn't threatened by the thought, but wanted to share in her insights. Just like that, his demeanor toward her began to change and she could feel it.

They kissed.

"What were we talking about?" he asked, bringing himself from her face.

"Your poems," she said softly. "What did you say you were writing about?"

My father, he thought to himself, but told a partial lie instead:“crack,” he laughed.

She cut him a disgusted face, “What?” she asked, her blonde brow folding in all over itself in confusion.

He laughed at her, citing this as the umpteenth pointless question of their night, “CRACK-COCAINE!” he blurted loudly, “… you know the other version of the shit you sell?”

She stared at him for a second, taken aback, and created some distance between them in his bed, “I’m sorry jeez… I didn’t know…what about it?”

He laughed at her again, his head bobbing steadily up and down, he knew that he had to find balance in his temperament towards her. He didn’t want to scare her away, “Don’t judge me…” he cackled, “… but it’s about white and black people.”

“What?”

"Black and White people and crack… flipping this shit to y'all I just see a ton of differences…"

She still didn't follow him and remained quiet in hopes that he would further explain himself.

He would. In fact, he was glad to and could feel all of the words settle neatly in his chest. He anticipated the catharsis he knew was to come, and in that moment, he prayed he wasn't too high to articulate exactly what he meant.

Even still, a smirk spread across his face before he opened his mouth to speak.

"Selling white-boys H and the blues, I just see a lot of differences and shit… like on the news and shit, how they talk about white fiends versus how they used to talk about us like back in the 90's with crack and shit… with you guys it's a disease now. With us it's more prison time," he started in…

She stared at him, wide-eyed, a pit growing in her stomach. And she didn't know why, but somehow, she felt personally attacked by his words. The whole time the words tumbled from his mouth, they fell on her ears abrasive and harsh. She knew she had to push down what she was feeling though—he was high and she already felt like she had to tip-toe around his unpredictable disposition already, which made her begin to question why she had stayed this long. She came over to Lee's place for the opposite of everything he had shown her tonight. She came to Lee's to escape Darius's stoicism, abrasion, and indifference. Lee was still in the game… and she liked that, but he was different in a manner she could never quite explain. Lee could though, he knew that she was only around him because he was a nigga, but not too much of one. Somehow, he was always the one whose black wasn't threatening, even despite his nappy hair, built physique, and near-purple skin. It was why the pink-toed fiends liked him he made them feel safe and assured. He made Hannah feel safe and assured. Just not tonight.

"Ya'll muhfukahs… ya'll muh…" he could barely manage, "ya'll get to hold out your arms outstretched like muhfucking Christ or something waiting on your next hit while we were always the ones kissing the ring… kissing that glass. They give ya'll rehab and probation we got ten more years," he scoffed.

His words went over her head, but she decided to hear him out and met him with more silence.

"All these white boys, they get to lay down in a field of poppy flowers when I serve em'," he murmured, his head fell back hard into the backboard but he continued on, aiming his diatribe at the dim and subdued ceiling now, "Black folk got to lay down on some hard ass rocks," he said. Head still held triumphantly upward, he trained his eyes on her; he wanted her to know that he was talking to her and only her.

She looked away from him.

"Even for you, you aint' gotta lay down on the rocks… you get to make angels in the snow… my dad didn't… my dad didn't…" he trailed off eyes closing shut.

She felt like crying.

He cried instead. His first instinct was not to let them come—the tears, he tried closing them even tighter but he couldn't hold them back. He finally allowed them to freely wash over his black cheeks and fall onto the white sheets. He thought up a white boy, gathering them up, collecting them from his eyes and, pouring them out onto a spoon, watering up their brown. He thought that…maybe his tears could serve some white boys when they went to draw up blood. He thought maybe that they could push his tears into their arms the way they did his H. He thought… and then he felt.

Hannah's arms wrapped around him now. His head dropped, tears falling onto her arms, leaving small tracks of warmth. She leaned in and kissed his cheek, desperate for some type of response, but he continued to lay stiff in her arms.

After some time, he pulled away from her, feeling returning to parts of his body in cold icy waves. He crawled down toward the edge of the bed avoiding eye contact with her. He had come down and wanted a high again.

"I gotta go. One sec..." he whispered before trotting off. He remembered the powder he had saved up from earlier and felt stupid for breaking another pill in half this go-round again. Still without a dollar, he did his best. Able to work out one large inhale as his head hovering awkwardly over his sink he ended up with about half of the blue dust in his nose and the other in the sink. Accepting as much of a victory as he could, he flushed the toilet, and returned to her.

"Come here," she endearingly commanded.

He did. Kneeling at the foot of the bed over her.

She wasn't afraid anymore. She shifted her weight, sheets tangling up around her left ankle as she took his face in her hands and kissed his lips. She felt their swell large and hot against hers and delighted having him this way again.

That embrace, warm and familial began to engulf him. It was coming on...

Her right hand fell from his face and slid down the length of his chest finally resting on his thigh.

He lifted his head upward, wanting to swallow up the taste of metal in his throat—hoping that the gravity would help push the drip down. His hands fumbled over hers recklessly at his zipper. She helped him, pulling down his pants to his waist his dick fell limply out; he was too high to get hard. When she tried bringing her lips to it, he thought of his father.

Kissing the glass.

Print Edition BONUS WORKS…

White Girl
Sparrow (Jesse Lane)

"American Gods" *(2016)*

Model: Que

White Girl
Sparrow (Jesse Lane)

"Spectre" *(2014)*

Mixed Media on Oriental Paper

White Girl
Sparrow (Jesse Lane)

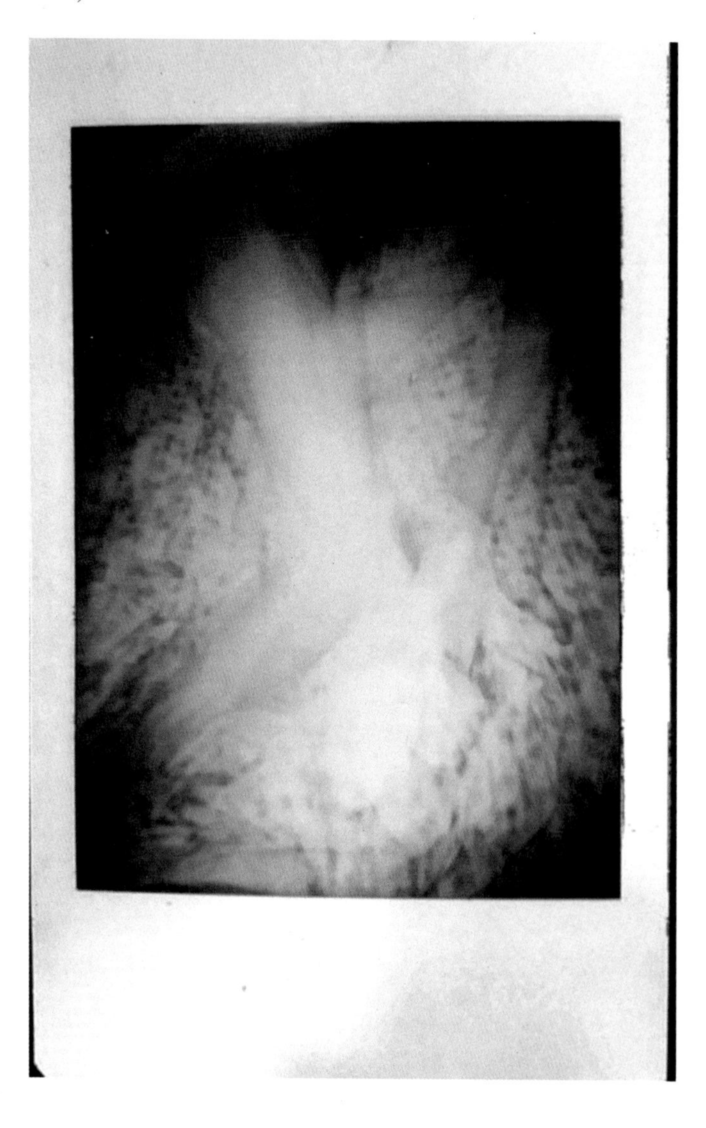

"White Girl" *(2016)*

Taken on Fujifilm Instax Film

"Lady Azul" *(2008)*

Mixed Media on Canvas

White Girl
Sparrow (Jesse Lane)

FINAL.

White Girl
Sparrow (Jesse Lane)

White Girl
Sparrow (Jesse Lane)

Made in the USA
Middletown, DE
14 November 2022